Calling All Engines!

A Random House PICTUREBACK® Book
Illustrated by Richard Courtney

Random House 🏠 New York

Thomas the Tank Engine & Friends®

A BRITT ALLCROFT COMPANY PRODUCTION

Based on The Railway Series by The Reverend W Awdry. © 2005 Gullane (Thomas) LLC.
Thomas the Tank Engine & Friends and Thomas & Friends are trademarks of Gullane Entertainment Inc.
Thomas the Tank Engine & Friends is Reg. U.S. Pat. TM Off.

A HIT Entertainment Company

www.randomhouse.com/kids/thomas   www.thomasandfriends.com

Library of Congress Control Number: 2005923708

ISBN 0-375-83119-3 Printed in the United States of America First Edition   15 14 13

Summer is a busy time on the Island of Sodor.

The engines love to show travelers around the island. They visit the seaside, the windmill, and the new Sodor Suspension Bridge.

One morning, Sir Topham Hatt came to the Shed. He had a very important announcement to make. "A new airport is to be built on Sodor and I need you all to help."

The engines were very excited.

Thomas and Percy were coupled to freight cars full
of bricks and timber to take to the airport building site.
"Imagine all the travelers," chuffed Thomas.
"And all the airplanes!" puffed Percy.

Then Arry and Bert arrived.

"Stinky steamies in the way again," mumbled Arry.

"Why do we have to work near them?" grumbled Bert.

This made Thomas and Percy cross. They didn't want to work near the diesels either. The diesels were oily, and they seemed very different to the steamies.

Thomas, Percy, Arry, and Bert worked at the airport all
afternoon. They shunted freight cars full of bricks and tar.
The diesels bumped Thomas and biffed Percy.
"Dirty diesels," moaned Percy. "I don't like them!"
Thomas and Percy had been so excited about working at the
airport, but Arry and Bert were there and now it wasn't any fun.

That night, a hurricane swept through the island. It was the
strongest wind the engines had ever known. All night long, the
wind howled down the tracks. It tore down the trees and ripped
off roofs.

The next morning, Thomas gasped at what he saw.
"Bust my buffers!" he cried. "Look at what the wind has done!"
The seaside had been battered, the windmill was wrecked, and
the Sodor Suspension Bridge had collapsed. Thomas felt terrible.

Sir Topham Hatt came to see the engines. "The hurricane has done lots of damage," he said sadly. "Everyone will have to work even harder if we want to open the airport."

Edward and Henry brought bricks to the airport building site while Diesel arrived with a load of timber.

But the diesels weren't talking to the steam engines, and the steam engines weren't talking to the diesels.

Everyone was cross.

That afternoon, Thomas had to collect some paint for
the bridge. He puffed into the builder's yard to pick up
the pots of paint.

But Diesel was in the yard, too. "Now I'll show Thomas
who's best," Diesel whispered. And he gave the freight cars
an extra-hard shunt. Paint pots flew into the air and
splattered down...

. . . all over Thomas!
Thomas looked very silly, indeed.
"Spotty boiler," laughed Diesel, and he rolled away.
"I'll show those diesels," Thomas huffed.

So the next time Thomas
saw Arry, he gave him a biff.

And when Arry saw James,
he gave him a bash.

Soon the diesels and the steamies were biffing and
banging and being bashed all over the island.

The engines were in a terrible mess, and no work had
been done.

That evening, Sir Topham Hatt came to see the engines. He was very angry. "You have caused confusion and delay. The seaside is still a mess. The bridge isn't painted. And we will not be able to open the airport. No travelers will come to Sodor this year!"

"No travelers," moaned Thomas.

"And no airplanes," groaned Percy.

All of the engines knew they had behaved badly, and they were very sad.

That night, Thomas had a dream. He was puffing along a misty mountain track. And there was Lady! Lady was a very special steam engine. She worked high up in the mountains.

Lady was shunting trucks with Rusty the diesel engine. Thomas was surprised.

"We always finish our jobs when we work together," puffed Lady.

The next morning when Thomas woke up, he had an idea.

First he went straight to see Mavis. Mavis was a kind diesel engine, and Thomas knew she would listen. He told Mavis that he wanted the steam engines and the diesels to work together.

Mavis agreed…it was the only way to get the airport open in time.

"Let's have a big meeting with all of the engines at the coaling stop tomorrow," Thomas puffed.

Thomas and Mavis went to see the other engines to tell them about the meeting.

Thomas told Percy…

Mavis told Diesel…

then James…

then Arry…

then Emily.

then Bert.

The next day, the engines gathered at the coaling stop. The steam engines and the diesels were all lined up. Thomas blew his whistle.

"Steamies and diesels need to work together," chuffed Thomas. "If the airport doesn't open, it will be bad for all the engines! Both steam engines and diesel engines need passengers and freight to be useful. If we work together, we can get the job done!" puffed Thomas.

All of the engines agreed.

After that, the engines worked harder than ever. They hauled bricks and timber and cleared away debris from the storm. They moved paint and tar and made sure there were enough workers to do each important job. And all the engines were careful not to bump or block each other. Even Diesel 10, the biggest diesel engine of all, agreed to help out! Soon the engines were even enjoying working together, smiling and joking as friends will do.

Before long, the airport was finished. It had shining buildings and a big tall control tower. And the runway was long and smooth. The engines were very proud. And very excited....

"I can't *wait* for the travelers," puffed Thomas.
"And look!" peeped Percy. "Here comes the first airplane."